Harry Potter
AND THE GOBLET OF FIRE™

MOVIE POSTER
BOOK

SCHOLASTIC INC.

New York   Toronto   London   Auckland   Sydney
Mexico City   New Delhi   Hong Kong   Buenos Aires

ISBN 0-439-63298-6

Published by Scholastic Inc. SCHOLASTIC and associated logos
are trademarks and/or registered trademarks of Scholastic Inc.

12 11 10 9 8 7 6 5 4 3 2 1   5 6 7 8 9/0

Designed by Two Red Shoes Design
Printed in the U.S.A.

First printing, November 2005

DANIEL RADCLIFFE

FACT-O-METER

Full name: Daniel Jacob Radcliffe

Harry Potter character: Harry Potter

Nickname: Dan (not Danny!)

Birthday: July 23, 1989

Astro sign: Cancer/Leo (on the cusp)

Chinese zodiac sign: snake

Eyes: blue

Hair: brown

Righty or lefty: right-handed

Pets: border terriers Binka and Nugget

Childhood dream job: fireman

First acting role: a monkey in a school play ("I had floppy ears and orange makeup and I had to wear tights. I think I went on and danced around for about 40 seconds or something. I hope nobody ever digs up a picture of me in that, because it would be embarrassing.")

TV credits: *David Copperfield* (British TV movie, 1999)

Movie credits: *Harry Potter and the Goblet of Fire* (2005); *Harry Potter and the Prisoner of Azkaban* (2004); *Harry Potter and the Chamber of Secrets* (2002); *Harry Potter and the Sorcerer's Stone* (2001); *The Tailor of Panama* (2001)

Fan mail: between 4,000–5,000 per month

Harry Potter stunt double: David Holmes ("He has been getting me to do gymnastics, body weights, press-ups, and chin-ups.")

Biggest fear: nuclear war

Places Daniel has visited: USA, Sweden, Spain, Italy, Holland, France, Japan, China, Australia

Places Daniel would like to visit: Russia, New Zealand, India

Charity: Demelza House Children's Hospice

Languages: Spanish

DANIEL'S FASCINATING FAVES

Music: ever-changing, but Daniel is into alternative and punk music
(*here's what's in his CD collection*):
Bloc Party
Blur
Kaiser Chiefs
The Libertines
The Futureheads
British Sea Power
Arcade Fire
Musical instrument: bass guitar, when he has time to practice
Musicians: Sid Vicious, Kim Deal (bass guitarist for the Pixies)
Beatles song: "Come Together" (Gary Oldman [Sirius Black] introduced
Daniel to the Beatles and they jammed on the song together.)
Personal sports: running and, most recently, scuba diving
Animal: wolf (". . . a beautiful animal and at the same time really dangerous")
Food: fish (especially sushi) or pizza
Soda: Diet Coke
Candy: Mars Bar
Dessert: vanilla ice cream with chocolate sauce; his least favorite dessert
is cake.
Snacks: Honey Nut Cheerios, a glass of milk with Jammy Dodgers Biscuits,
salty popcorn
Cold-weather drink: hot chocolate
Holiday: Christmas
Season of the year: summer ("I've finished my exams and it's warm and hot
and I have more time to hang out with my friends.")
Movies: *The Edukators, Good Bye Lenin!, Eternal Sunshine of the Spotless
Mind, Mystic River*
All-time movie: *12 Angry Men*
TV shows: *The Simpsons* ("I can quote scenes from *The Simpsons!*")
Simpsons character: Bart Simpson
Old British TV show: *Dad's Army*
Classical play: Shakespeare's *A Midsummer Night's Dream*; "I would like to
play Puck."

Books: *1984* by George Orwell, *The War of Don Emmanuel's Nether Parts* by Louis de Bernières, *Three Men in a Boat* by Jerome K. Jerome

Harry Potter book: *Harry Potter and the Prisoner of Azkaban*

Harry Potter characters: Sirius Black, Hagrid, and the Weasleys

Harry Potter word: "Voldemort"

Harry Potter magic ability: invisibility

Harry Potter special-effects scenes: Quidditch ("It's very surreal playing Quidditch!")

Harry Potter prop: Godric Gryffindor's sword

Harry Potter animal: Gizmo (the owl that plays Hedwig)

Actors: Gary Oldman, Tom Hanks, Ben Stiller, Jude Law, Ed Harris, Robert DeNiro

Actresses: Nicole Kidman, Julia Roberts, Kate Winslet, Kirsten Dunst, Cameron Diaz, Scarlett Johansson

Colors: yellow and blue

Number: seven

Superhero: Spider-Man

School subjects: English Literature, History, Religion

Style of writing: poetry

Way to relax: "I like to just lock myself up in a small room and listen to music and watch films for a day."

Video game system: PlayStation 2

Video games: Medal of Honor, The Simpsons Road Rage, and games based on the NFL and the NBA

High-tech gadget: iPod

Never-leave-home-without gadget: portable DVD player

Style of clothing: casual ("I have hundreds and hundreds of T-shirts.")

T-shirt designer: Burro and Louis Epstein

Place in London: Camden Market ("It's a very cool place to shop with a lot of good music stores.")

Historical spot in London: The Tower of London

Roller coasters: Dragon Kahn in Barcelona, Spain (it has eight 360-degree loops) and Disney's Space Mountain

Fantasy car: Red Cadillac from *Fear and Loathing in Las Vegas*

Place he visited: China (He walked on the Great Wall of China in the snow!)

DANIEL ON HARRY

Would he be friends with Harry in real life?

"Absolutely. I like his curiosity and his loyalty. And his magic powers, too. He's so serious, but at the same time he can be very funny."

What does he admire about Harry?

"I think the reason everybody identifies with him is because — other than that he's a wizard — he's a really normal person. Harry goes from being a zero to a hero — he goes from being nothing to somebody really huge and famous and very important in the wizard world. I think he has inspired a lot of people, including me."

How does he get into the state of mind to play Harry?

"Harry, being a teenager, has the same feelings as every other teenager. But because of his past, I think he feels these feelings of anger or loneliness. Because of his past, I think he feels more strongly. So that was hard for me, but because I obviously am feeling the same things as him, I just took what I was feeling and basically exaggerated it and listened to music or anything to get me into the right state of mind for the filming. And then just hoped for the best once I was in there really."

What do wizard robes feel like?

"[Really] comfy. They feel kind of like pajamas. They were only hot during the Great Hall scenes because there were huge fires all around."

Is he like Harry?

"I'm quite like him. Harry's so multidimensional that everyone can find something in themselves that Harry has, too. He's not one of those haughty superheroes."

What are the best and worst parts of playing Harry?

"The best part of playing Harry is seeing the finished film. After having worked on the film for 10 months, it is fantastic to see it complete. At the moment there is no worst bit. I don't think anyone believes me, but there really isn't!"

DANIEL FINISHES THE SENTENCE

If I go to college . . . "I would probably like to study psychology."

Since Harry Potter, my friends have been . . . "absolutely fantastic. There's no jealousy or anything like that. Everyone's been really nice."

As far as dating goes . . . "I am flattered by fan letters, it's really amazing. But I don't have a girlfriend or anything."

If I could play another Harry Potter character . . . "it would be Gilderoy Lockhart. He's a showoff, but also he's a coward. He would be really funny to play . . . or Sirius, as I am intrigued about the relationship he has with Harry and his father."

My least favorite kind of food . . . "is junk food."

If I could change one thing in the world . . . "I would bring John Lennon back, as I think he was a genius."

If I could go anywhere in the world . . . "I would love to go on a mountain expedition to say, Everest, and make an attempt at that."

The hardest thing about scuba diving is . . . "you really need to pee all the time! You know, surrounded by all that water . . . "

If I could play a character in *Lord of the Rings* . . . "it would be Gollum."

For the Harry Potter movies I'm in the makeup room for . . . "about thirty minutes because of the scar."

When I grow up, I might be . . . "a writer or I might like to be a director."

I have always . . . "believed in magic, a hundred percent. I'm fascinated by it."

On being afraid: "I get a bit claustrophobic at times. And I don't like snakes and spiders much."

On being shy: "I am a shy person. But I'm not really shy in front of the camera, though, because I'm not playing me. I'm playing a different person."

On loving punk music: "One of the crew members on Harry Potter got me into the whole punk thing. He introduced me to the music and the clothes and told me stories about the bands and that got me started."

On girls being attracted to him: "Um, maybe a bit, yeah. I'm not complaining."

On when he learned he won the role of Harry Potter: "I was in the bath at the time and my dad picked up the phone. I heard him say 'Hello, David!' . . . My dad came upstairs and I thought that it was going to be a letdown call to say that I didn't get the part. But he came upstairs and told me and I just sat there for a while to just let it sink in. . . . I just started to cry because I was so happy."

On the infamous "towel girl": "I was doing MTV in New York [to promote *Harry Potter and the Sorcerer's Stone*]. And it was freezing cold out. I mean, it's not like it was a warm summer's day. It was so cold. And I got up and they took me over to the window [overlooking Times Square]. And there was a girl standing down there wearing nothing but a Harry Potter towel with a sign that said, 'It doesn't get much better than this.' And with another sign that said, 'Nothing comes between me and Harry Potter.' It was great!"

On how he acted in the Dobby scenes: "I loved doing the Dobby scenes. I talked to an orange ball at the end of a stick. It was very detailed work because as he bounced around, I had to ensure that my eyeline was in exactly the right position. It was demanding, but when I saw the end result, I was really pleased."

EMMA WATSON

THE BASICS

Full name: Emma Charlotte Duerre Watson

Harry Potter character: Hermione Granger

Nickname: Em

Harry Potter nickname: One-Take Watson

Birthday: April 15, 1990

Astro sign: Aries

Eyes: brown

Hair: blond (although she's a brunette for the *Harry Potter* films)

Pets: cats Bubbles and Domino (Domino is really her brother's cat.)

First acting roles: school plays, *Arthur: The Younger Years; The Swallow and the Prince; The Happy Prince; Alice in Wonderland*

First competition: The Daisy Pratt Poetry Competition (a school poetry recital in which she won first place)

First book read: *The Very Hungry Caterpillar* by Eric Carle

Movie credits: *Harry Potter and the Goblet of Fire* (2005); *Harry Potter and the Prisoner of Azkaban* (2004); *Harry Potter and the Chamber of Secrets* (2002); *Harry Potter and the Sorcerer's Stone* (2001)

Harry Potter auditions: selected over thousands of young actresses (many of whom had extensive professional credentials)

Awards: Best Performance by a Youth – Female: Phoenix Film Critics' Society; Best Supporting Actress – AOL Moviegoer Awards

Best gift received: a CD player

What makes her smile on cue: "You just have to think of a happy thought."

EMMA'S FUN-TASTIC FAVES

Color: blue

Lip gloss: Stila

Gadget: iPod

Cell phone: Sony Ericsson

Animal: cat

Food: anything on toast; Murray Mints

Snack: chocolate

Candy: lemon sherbet jelly beans

Designers: DKNY, Agnes B, Nicole Farhi, Marc Jacobs, Alberta Ferretti

Pastimes: shopping, talking on the phone, and e-mailing friends

Musicians: her dad's collection of Eric Clapton, BB King, John Hiatt, Bryan Adams, Steely Dan, and Lloyd Cole; her mum's collection of the Pretenders, Tina Turner, Celine Dion; "chicks with guitars" type music; hip-hop; R&B; listening to Capital Radio . . . almost anything!

Actors: John Cleese

Actresses: Julia Roberts, Sandra Bullock, Goldie Hawn, Natalie Portman, Nicole Kidman, and Cate Blanchett

Movies: *The Shawshank Redemption, Gladiator, Braveheart, Pride and Prejudice, Grease, Shrek (1* and *2)*

Sports: hockey, tennis, rounders, netball, athletics, and track events

Vacation sports: parasailing and water-skiing

Games: card games such as Spit, Slam, and Snap

School subjects: Art, History, English (dislikes Math and Geography)

Extracurricular subjects: debating and poetry

Magic power: invisibility

Harry Potter character: Hagrid

Harry Potter book: *Harry Potter and the Prisoner of Azkaban*

Harry Potter set: the chessboard set from *Harry Potter and the Sorcerer's Stone*

Harry Potter house: Gryffindor (of course!)

Books: *The Phantom Tollbooth* by Norton Juster, *I Capture the Castle* by Dodie Smith, *Noughts and Crosses* by Malorie Blackman, *His Dark Materials* by Philip Pullman, *The Islanders* by Roland Pertwee

Author: Roald Dahl

RON WEASLEY
RUPERT GRINT

HEAD-TO-TOE

Full name: Rupert Alexander Grint
Harry Potter character: Ron Weasley
Nickname: Rupe
Birthday: August 24, 1988
Astro sign: Virgo
Eyes: blue
Hair: red
Pets: Ruby, black Labrador, and Fudge, chocolate lab
First acting roles: school productions and local theater productions: "In *Noah's Ark*, I was a fish. In the nativity play, I think I was a donkey. *Cinderella*, I was just a chorus thing. And *Rumplestiltskin*, I was Rump."
First book read: *Each Peach Pear Plum* by Allan Ahlberg and Janet Ahlberg
Movie credits: *Harry Potter and the Goblet of Fire* (2005); *Harry Potter and the Prisoner of Azkaban* (2004); *Harry Potter and the Chamber of Secrets* (2002); *Thunderpants* (2002); *Harry Potter and the Sorcerer's Stone* (2001)
Where he was when he got the role of Ron: with Emma Watson when director Chris Columbus and producer David Heyman told them both they were cast in the movie
Scariest Harry Potter character: "For me, Hermione! Just kidding. Voldemort!"
Childhood dream job: ice-cream man
Foreign language: German
Pet peeves: vegetables
Biggest fear: spiders and the dark
What makes him act scared on cue: "I think of something scary, like maybe a teacher I had. Although then I might get too scared!"
Most embarrassing moment: "I drew a picture of Alan Rickman [Professor Snape]. It was kind of amazing, but really ugly. Then I found out that he was right behind me, watching me draw this picture. He took it really well."
Coolest thing he's bought: quad bike
Childhood collection: yo-yos (his favorite was the Super Yo Satellite)

RUPERT'S RAVES

Gadget: Sony Viao laptop
Cell phone: Motorola v3
Article of clothing: jeans
Cartoon character: SpongeBob SquarePants
Music: rock
Movies: *The Life Aquatic with Steve Zissou, Star Wars*
Snacks: "Sweets!"
Food: burger
Late-night snack: ice cream
Birthday present: unicycle for his 14th birthday
Car: hot rod
Sports: football, rugby, golf
Sports team: Tottenham Hotspur (The Spurs) soccer team
Pastimes: golf, sleeping
School subjects: Art
Video game format: GameCube and PlayStation 2
Video game: Need for Speed
Catchphrase: "wicked"
Kinds of books: comedy and horror
Books: Darren Shan's Cirque Du Freak series and *Of Mice and Men* by
    John Steinbeck
Author: J. K. Rowling
Harry Potter books: *Harry Potter and the Prisoner of Azkaban* and *Harry
    Potter and the Goblet of Fire*
Harry Potter scenes: the chess scene in *Sorcerer's Stone*; the slug scene in
    Chamber of Secrets; the flying car when they bashed into the willow
    tree in *Chamber of Secrets*
Harry Potter character: Ron
Harry Potter character Rupert would like to play: "Malfoy. He's pretty nasty at
    times and that would be quite fun. It would be cool to have the
    audience against me."
Harry Potter animal: Scabbers (Ron's rat; his real name is Mosh Pit)
Harry Potter line of dialogue: "Bloody brilliant!"
Magic powers: Flying car – no traffic!
Tourist visit in New York: the Empire State Building

DRACO MALFOY
TOM FELTON

Full name: Thomas Andrew Felton

Harry Potter character: Draco Malfoy

Nickname: Tom

Birthday: September 22, 1987

Astro sign: Virgo

Eyes: blue

Hair: brownish-blond

Height: 5'9"

Childhood pets: rabbits and a chinchilla

First professional job: commercial campaign

TV credits: *Second Sight II: Hide and Seek* (2000); *Second Sight* (1999); *Bugs* (1995)

Movie credits: *Harry Potter and the Goblet of Fire* (2005); *Harry Potter and the Prisoner of Azkaban* (2004); *Harry Potter and the Chamber of Secrets* (2002); *Harry Potter and the Sorcerer's Stone* (2001); *Anna and the King* (1999); *The Borrowers* (1997)

Scariest Harry Potter moment: seeing the Dementors in *Prisoner of Azkaban* ("I've seen some of the suits they wear and they frighten me. You wouldn't want to see one out and about — that's for sure.")

Description of Draco: "Draco's not really a bully. He's not exactly the biggest, strongest guy in the world. He's more a rich, snobby person. He thinks of himself as really cool."

Self-made sandwich: "About three rashers [slices] of bacon, a massive burger, a couple of sausages, and a fried egg. It's very fatty and not very healthy for you, but I'm sure it would taste absolutely gorgeous."

Amazing fact: didn't read any of the Harry Potter books until after he filmed *Chamber of Secrets*

Country: England

Cities in America: New York, NY; Waddington, NY

Sports: basketball, soccer, ice-skating, Rollerblading, cricket, swimming, tennis

Newest passion: fishing ("I only fish for carp using the catch-and-release system so that the fish are never hurt. My biggest fish was a common carp caught on the beautiful river of St. Lawrence in Waddington in New York State, USA. It weighed 16.88 kilos [37 pounds].")

Pastime: shopping ("I'm obsessed with shopping! Occasionally I'll get these little urges to buy, like to shop for stuff on the Internet. I search for all kinds of weird gizmos.")

Prized possession: Kona bike

Style of clothing: casual – big sweatshirts

TV shows: *The Simpsons, EastEnders* (British TV)

Music: rap, hip-hop

Musicians: Tupac Shakur, Big Syke

Actor: Samuel L. Jackson

Book: Darren Shan's Cirque Du Freak series

Magic power: "To make the world silent."

Harry Potter house: Slytherin

Harry Potter character: Lucius Malfoy

Childhood book: *The Snowman* by R. L. Stine

Food: "I like plain food with no spices or herbs or onions. Favorite foods are cream crackers, chocolate ice cream without any bits, pepperoni pizza without onions, chicken, Mum's Shepherd's Pie, Tesco's frozen plain sausages, pancakes, and of course chocolate!"

Fast food: hamburgers, pizza

Sweets: chocolate

Drink: chocolate milk

Relaxation: reading

Colors: car, black and white; envelopes, red; clothes, gray

Car: BMW

Designers: Armani, Versace

School subjects: Geography, English, Physics

Villain in a movie: Alan Rickman in *Robin Hood: Prince of Thieves*

JOSHUA HERDMAN   JAMIE WAYLETT

JOSHUA FACTS

Full name: Joshua Herdman
Nickname: Josh
Harry Potter character: Gregory Goyle
Height: 6'4"
TV credit: *UGetMe* (series) (2003);
the BBC's *Dad*; ITV's *The Bill*
Movie credits: *Harry Potter and the
Goblet of Fire* (2005); *Harry
Potter and the Prisoner of
Azkaban* (2004); *Harry Potter
and the Chamber of Secrets*
(2002); *Thunderpants* (2002);
*Harry Potter and the Sorcerer's
Stone* (2001)

JAMIE FACTS

Name: Jamie Waylett
Harry Potter character:
Vincent Crabbe
Nickname: Jay
Birthday: July 21, 1989
Astro sign: Cancer
Eyes: brown
Hair: brown
Pets: goldfish named Angel
Movie credits: *Harry Potter and the
Goblet of Fire* (2005); *Harry
Potter and the Prisoner of
Azkaban* (2004); *Harry Potter
and the Chamber of Secrets*
(2002); *Harry Potter and the
Sorcerer's Stone* (2001)
Harry Potter audition: first considered
for the role of Dudley Dursley
(Harry's spoiled cousin), but
director Chris Columbus decided
to have him audition for the role
of Vincent Crabbe
Childhood trauma: When Jamie was
9 years old, he was hit by a car
and wasn't expected to live. After
four days unconscious Jamie
woke up. He spent 9 months
recuperating, but recovered
completely!

KATIE LEUNG

THE FACT SHEET

Full name: Katie Leung

Harry Potter character: Cho Chang

Birthday: August 8, 1987

Astro sign: Leo

Movie credit: *Harry Potter and the Goblet of Fire* (2005)

Fun fact: Katie beat out more than 3,000 girls for the role of Cho Chang.

Friend's description of Katie: Katie is a very loyal friend who has a bubbly personality. She has a unique dress sense.

VIKTOR KRUM
STANISLAV IANEVSKI

EVERYTHING YOU NEED TO KNOW

Name: Stanislav Ianevski
Nickname: Stan
Harry Potter character: Viktor Krum
Birthday: May 16, 1985
Astro sign: Taurus
Pets: A parrot, a cat, two dogs and a guinea pig family

STANISLAV'S MUST-HAVE FAVES

Hobby: Gym training
Sports team: Bulgarian National Football team
Musicians or bands: all kinds, especially Bulgarian music
Food: Bulgarian dishes and anything sweet!
Films: *XXX, The Last Samurai, Lord of the Rings* trilogy and all the *Harry Potter* films!
Actor/actress: Keanu Reeves, Vin Diesel, Angelina Jolie and Liv Tyler
Favorite place visited: Has traveled all of his life but Bulgaria would come first!
Acting credits: *Harry Potter and the Goblet of Fire* (2005)

JAMES & OLIVER PHELPS

JAMES FACTS

Full name: James Andrew Eric Phelps
Harry Potter character: Fred Weasley
Birthday: February 25, 1986
Astro sign: Pisces
Height: 6'3"
Eyes: brown
Hair: brown (not red!)
Identifying mark: scar on his right cheek
Pets: bearded collies Ewan and Rupert
Person he most admires: Winston Churchill
Musicians: Foo Fighters, Bon Jovi, Red Hot Chili Peppers, Muse, Queen, Green Day, Coldplay, Metallica, AC/DC, The Beatles, Guns 'n Roses, Velvet Revolver, Led Zeppelin
Style of music: rock, hard rock, metal
Movie: *Forrest Gump* or *Happy Gilmore*
Color: blue
Sports: soccer, golf, snooker, and bowling
School subjects: English, Business Studies, Drama
Harry Potter book: *Harry Potter and the Prisoner of Azkaban*
Magic power: "I'd like to be invisible — can you imagine how much you could get away with if you could turn invisible!?"

OLIVER FACTS

Full name: Oliver Martyn John Phelps
Harry Potter character: George Weasley
Birthday: February 25, 1986
Astro sign: Pisces
Height: 6'3"
Eyes: brown
Hair: brown (not red!)
Identifying mark: mole at the top of his nose
First acting roles: school productions
High school: Arthur Terry School (graduated in 2004)
Person he most admires: Richard Branson (CEO/founder of Virgin Airways)
Musicians: Foo Fighters, Coldplay, Red Hot Chili Peppers, Creed, Queen, Muse, Green Day, Velvet Revolver
Style of music: rock
Movie: *The Incredibles*
Color: red
Sports: soccer, golf
Sports teams: Aston Villa (the rival team of James's faves, Birmingham Blues)
Harry Potter book: *Harry Potter and the Goblet of Fire*
Magic power: "To fly. I would love to be up in the air and looking at what's going on down below."
Clothing store he likes to shop: Bull Ring in Birmingham

CLÉMENCE POÉSY

MINI-BIO

Name: Clémence Poésy

Harry Potter character: Fleur Delacour

Birth year: 1982

Birthplace: Paris, France

TV credits: *Gunpowder, Treason and Plot* (2004); *La vie quand même* (2003); *Tania Boréalis* (2001)

Movie credits: *Harry Potter and the Goblet of Fire* (2005); *Olgas Sommer* (2003); *Bienvenue chez les Roses* (2003); *Petite soeur* (2001)

In production: *Revelations, Mon Prisonnier*, and *Les Animaux Domestiques*

How she got into acting: Her father is a theater director and actor.

ROBERT PATTINSON

mini-bio

Name: Robert Pattinson
Harry Potter character: Cedric Diggory
Birthplace: London, England
Birth year: 1987
Height: 6'1"
Sports: soccer, skiing, snowboarding
Instruments: guitar, keyboards
School theater club: Barnes Theatre Club
Theater credits: *Macbeth; Anything Goes; Tess of the D'Urbervilles; Our Town*
TV credit: *Ring of the Nibelungs* (2004)
Movie credits: *Harry Potter and the Goblet of Fire* (2005); *Vanity Fair* (2004)

MATTHEW LEWIS

FACTS, FACTS, FACTS

Name: Matthew Lewis

Harry Potter character: Neville Longbottom

Birthdate: June 27, 1989

Astro sign: Cancer

Hobby: reading (especially Darren Shan and J. K. Rowling books) and football (soccer)

Pastime: video games like Tiger Woods PGA Tour, FIFA Football, Pro Revolution Soccer, Killzone, Grand Theft Auto, Call of Duty

Sports: soccer and rugby league

Favorite teams: Leeds United (soccer) and Leeds Rhinos (rugby)

Favorite musicians: Green Day, Red Hot Chili Peppers, The Strokes, The Killers, Coldplay, Guns 'n Roses, Velvet Revolver, Embrace

Favorite actor/actress: Al Pacino and Kate Beckinsale

Favorite film: *Interview with the Vampire*

Clothing store he likes to shop: French Connection UK

TV credits: *Heartbeat* (YTV) (1999); *Big Bag* (YTV) (1999); *Big Bag* (YTV) (1998); *City Central* (BBC) (1997); *Dalziel and Pascoe: An Advancement of Learning* (1996); *Where the Heart Is* (YTV) (1996); *Some Kind of Life* (1995)

Movie credits: *Harry Potter and the Goblet of Fire* (2005); *Harry Potter and the Prisoner of Azkaban* (2004); *Harry Potter and the Chamber of Secrets* (2002); *Harry Potter and the Sorcerer's Stone* (2001)